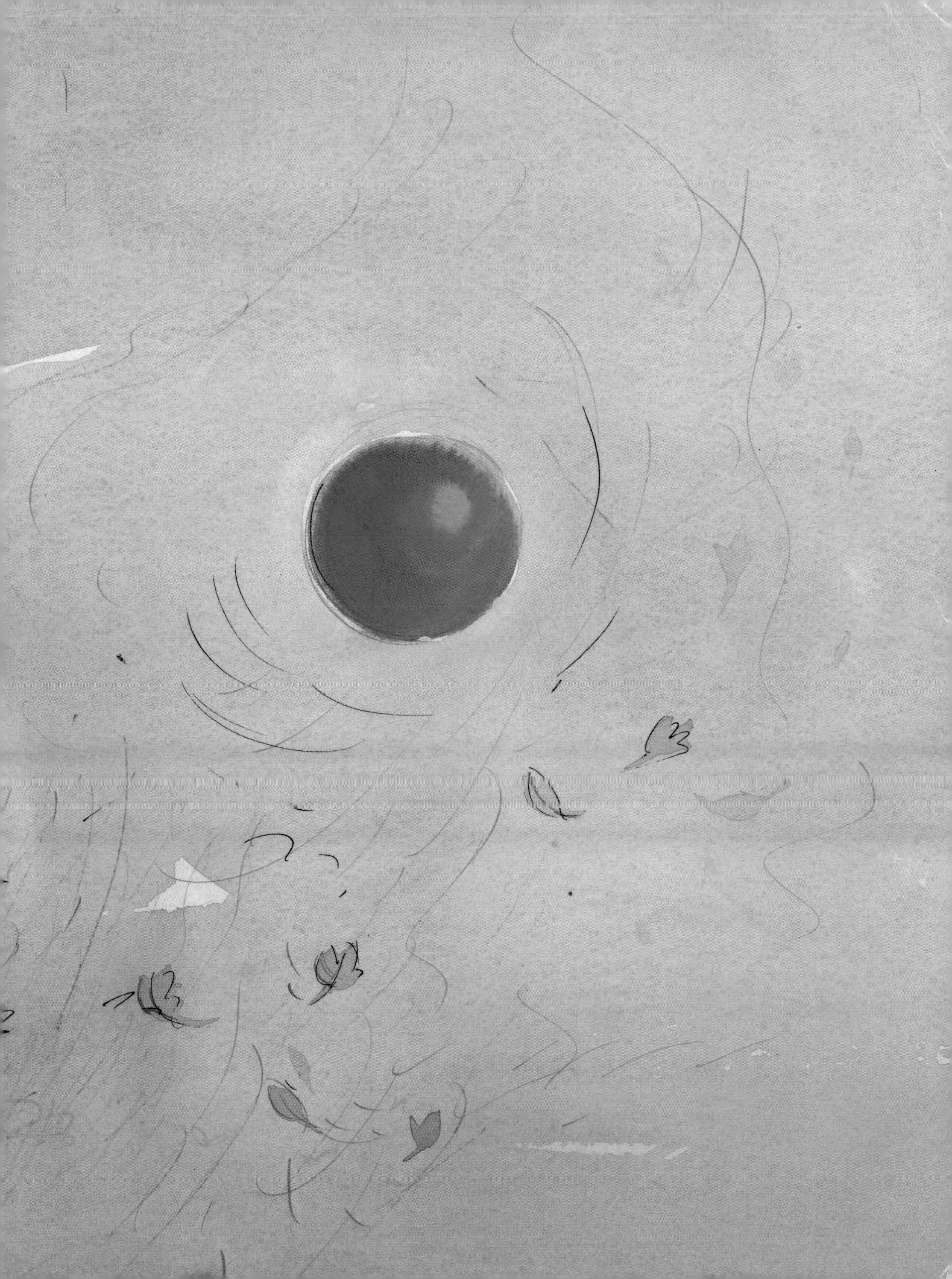

To grandfathers everywhere A.B.H.

For Katy R.B.C.

OXFORD
UNIVERSITY PRESS

Great Clarendon Street, Oxford OX2 6DP

Oxford University Press is a department of the University of Oxford.
It furthers the University's objective of excellence in research, scholarship,
and education by publishing worldwide in

Oxford New York

Athens Auckland Bangkok Bogotá Buenos Aires Calcutta
Cape Town Chennai Dar es Salaam Delhi Florence Hong Kong Istanbul
Karachi Kuala Lumpur Madrid Melbourne Mexico City Mumbai
Nairobi Paris São Paulo Singapore Taipei Tokyo Toronto Warsaw

with associated companies in Berlin Ibadan

First published 2000

British Library Cataloguing in Publication Data available

ISBN 0-19-279014-5 (hardback)
ISBN 0-19-272334-0 (paperback)

Typeset by Branka Surla
Printed in Hong Kong

Hold My Hand, Grandpa

Ann Bixby Herold
Illustrated by Robin Bell Corfield

OXFORD
UNIVERSITY PRESS

Grandpa was there when Holly took her first steps.
'Come to me, Holly, I won't let you fall.'

On his next visit, he walked her round the house.

Boodle lolloped along behind, nudging Holly with his nose.

'Boodle is helping you learn to walk, too,' said Grandpa.

Grandpa was there when Holly walked, by herself, across the lawn.

‘Oops-a-daisy,’ he said when she sat, giggling, in a clump of daisies.

‘Hold my hand, and let’s walk over to the patio. Here comes Mummy.’

As Holly grew bigger she learned how to

go up and down stairs

climb out of the bath

ride a tricycle

run races with Boodle.

She moved to a big bed, because only babies need a cot. When Mummy said, 'Into bed with you,' Holly didn't need help.

But if Grandpa was there, she always asked him to tuck her in.

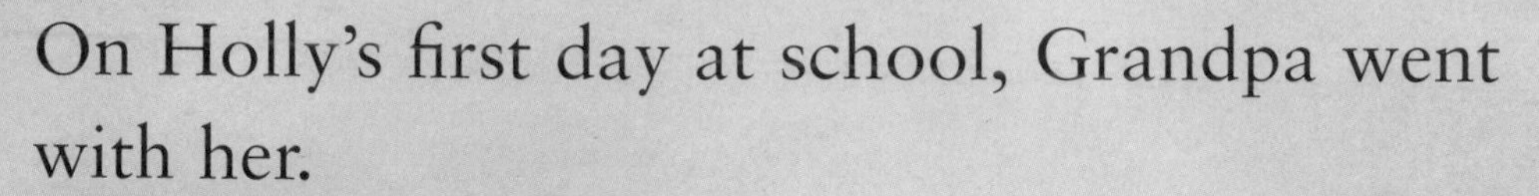

On Holly's first day at school, Grandpa went with her.

'Hold my hand while we cross the road, Holly.'

She slipped her hand into his big, rough one. It reminded her of when she was little, and made her feel safe.

Grandpa came to meet her from school, Boodle tucked under his arm. Grandpa gave her a kiss. So did Boodle.

'Hold my hand, Holly.'

She sighed. 'It's too far to walk, Grandpa. My legs are tired.'

'It's been a long day,' he said. 'Would you like a piggyback ride?'

Grandpa carried Holly all the way home.

After a while, the walk home from school didn't seem so far. Especially when Grandpa came to meet her.

There was a lot to tell as Boodle tugged them home to tea. Sometimes, if she was extra tired, she asked Grandpa to carry her.

'You are too big now, Holly,' he said.

When Holly learned to ride a two-wheeler,
Grandpa was there.

'Hold on, Holly. I won't let you fall off.'

One day Grandpa started limping.

Then he couldn't walk at all.

Holly went to visit him in the hospital.

'I've got a new hip,' he told her. 'I'm coming to stay with you until I'm better.'

Soon, Grandpa was able to meet her from school in a wheelchair. 'I'm still learning to walk again, and it's too far for me,' he said.

'Giddy-up, Boodle!' said Holly. 'Hold on tight, Grandpa!'

When Grandpa was well enough to go to his own house, Holly said, 'I'll help you up the steps. Hold my hand, Grandpa. I won't let you fall.'

She led him indoors.

'Surprise!'

A NEW HIP. HOORAY! said the icing on the cake.

At Grandpa's place there was a long present, wrapped in bright paper.

'It's for when I'm not there to hold your hand,' said Holly.

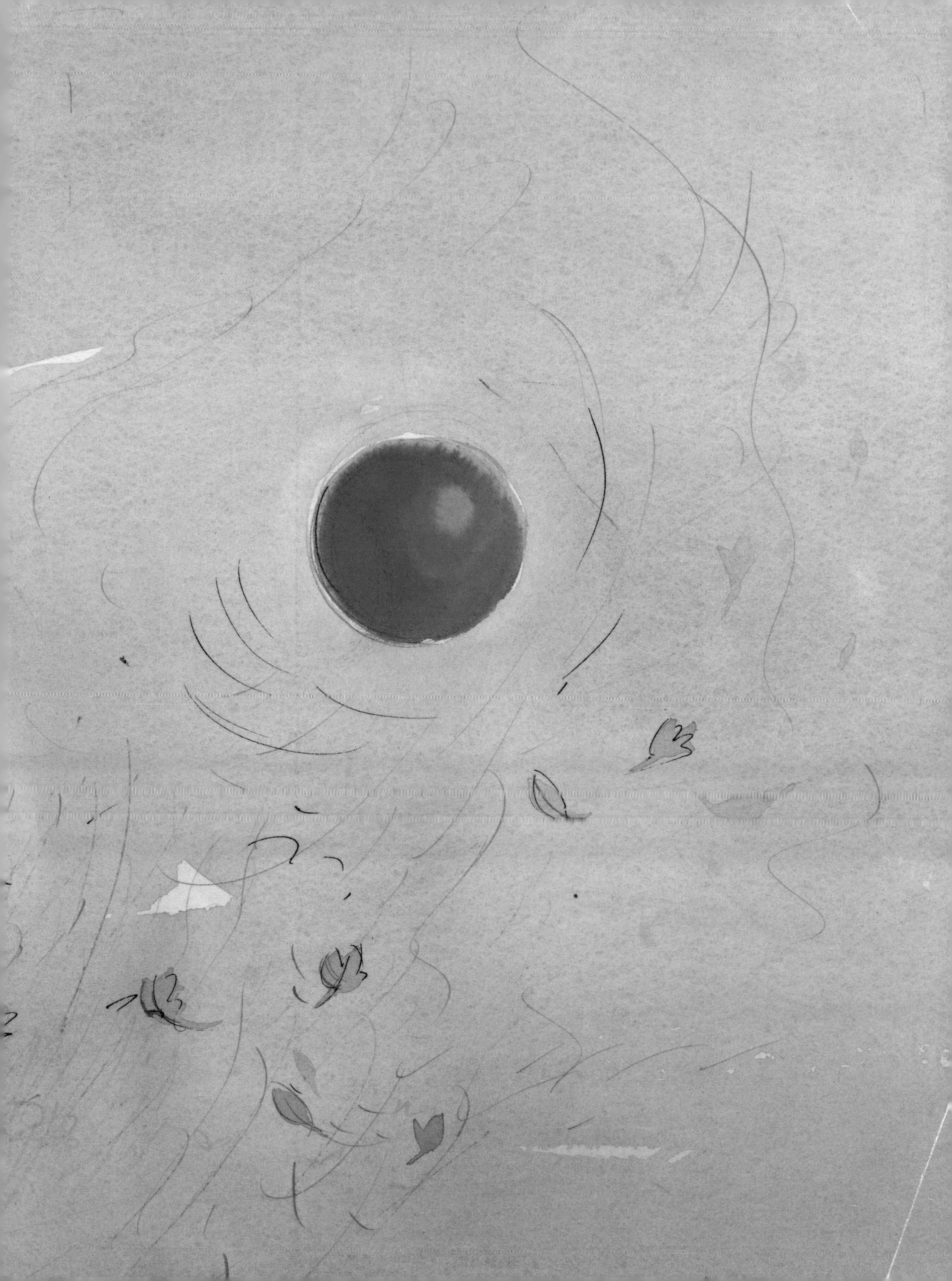